# Close-Up

# Close-Up

SZABINKA DUDEVSZKY

PHOTOGRAPHS: PIETER KERS
TRANSLATION: WANDA BOEKE

Front Street & Lemniscaat
Asheville, North Carolina
1999

*With thanks to all the young people,
(foster) parents, social workers, caretakers,
and Monique Steenstra.*

Library of Congress Catalog-in-Publication Data
Dudevszky, Szabinka, 1964-
[Close-Up. English]
Close-Up / Szabinka Dudevszky; photographs by Pieter Kers;
translation by Wanda Boeke
p. cm.
Summary: Fifteen self-portraits of young people in the Netherlands who for various
reasons cannot live with their parents, including those who have been physically or
emotionally abused, those who have run away, and those in foster homes.
ISBN 1-886910-40-5
1. Foster children–Netherlands–Juvenile literature.
2. Runaway children–Netherlands–Juvenile literature.
3. Abused children–Netherlands–Juvenile literature.
[1. Child abuse. 2. Foster home care. 3. Runaways.]
I. Kers, Pieter, ill. II. Title
HV887.N4D8313   1999
362.7' 09492–dc21                    98-45085

# Close-Up

# Contents

# On My Own

At school I was a disaster. I think I bothered a lot of people. A group of us from the neighborhood went to a vocational junior high school on the outskirts of the city. On the streetcar on our way to school we would already be acting up. Boombox, mouthing off to strangers, dancing. That kind of thing. At school we just kept it up. Being pains, throwing apples, hassling people. On the way home a boy and I'd smash streetcar shelters. I couldn't have cared less about anything. As long as I didn't have to go home.

## Delinquents

At home I always fought with my father. He wanted to lay down rules for everything: where I went, who I hung out with. If he didn't like one of my friends, I could forget about seeing her. I wouldn't be allowed to go over to her house. He had very strict rules. Be home at five o'clock every day. No way he'd let me go out, go into the city with friends. He thought that kind of thing was for delinquents.

At one point something happened to my father's leg and he wasn't allowed to work anymore. He got moody, couldn't handle anything. I think he felt useless. He started drinking too. He was always checking up on where I'd been. If I came home late, he'd be waiting for me. Then he'd beat me, with his hands or with a belt, whatever was handy.

## Having Weird Thoughts

At school nobody knew anything, nobody asked about anything. They just thought I was a pain. Sometimes I'd have welts on my arms and legs. I'd hide them under my clothes. One time when I was desperate I told a teacher something. But he never asked me about it afterward.

A couple of friends knew what was going on. They could tell by my face if I was in a bad mood, if there had been another fight. But what could they do? Some of them had problems of their own.

At night in my room I'd start having these weird thoughts. I hoped something would happen to my father, that he'd die. I'd fantasize about that. The next morning I'd be crying again. I would feel so ashamed. I can't be

doing that, I'd think, he is my father after all.

I see it like this: whatever I couldn't get off my chest at home, I'd vent at school. After six months they'd had enough of me there. I fought with a girl on the streetcar and was kicked out of school. I felt really bad then, you know. I decided I'd change how I acted. Luckily I knew a couple of people at my new school and made friends quickly. Fighting wasn't part of the picture anymore. I passed into ninth grade with B's and A's.

But things at home I couldn't change. It seemed like my father couldn't stand my having fun. He kept dreaming up new ways to torment me. For example, I was part of a dance group at school and was going to be in a performance. At the last minute he wouldn't let me take part in it. I thought that was so mean.

## Cape Verde

Sometimes I wonder how come my father acted like that. He was also hard on my brothers and sisters. But they stuck to the rules, didn't stand up to him.

My father grew up in Cape Verde and was raised with the belt. He thinks beating goes along with raising children. But I was born here. I think that if something's wrong, you can talk about it. That's what I wanted most: for him to talk to me, for us to do things together. It's not that I wanted a different father, I wanted him to act different.

I don't blame my mother for anything. If my father hit

me, she'd try to stop him. But she never talked about it. I thought that was a mistake. Even if she'd just asked, "Hey, Manuela, how you doing?"

## Everything Went Wrong

When I was fifteen, everything went wrong. A friend of mine was raped by her own father. I knew her father, I never thought he'd do something like that. My friend looked awful. We both went to file a complaint with the police and she was taken in by friends. I was totally messed up by it. At home they had no idea. At school either. I had nobody to talk to about things like that.

Not long after that I also ran away. I had a huge fight with my father. He claimed I had taken money out of his bank account. It wasn't true. But he kept on, for two weeks. I told him to stop, that I really hadn't done it. He became furious and started to hit me. The next day I went to the police. I was scared, but I thought: you have to do this, otherwise you'll never get away from him. They were very kind at the police station. I told them everything and they sent me to the Child Welfare office.

Some kids say that everything gets solved when you run away. Staying overnight with one person, then another, having fun, not going to school. But this doesn't get you anywhere. You have to look for people you can trust, who can help you. First I was taken in by a friend and her parents. Then I stayed with a woman and her children for two years. Those people were good to me. I received the most support from my youth counselor. She talked with me a lot, I could tell her anything. And she was sincere. She really wanted things to get better for me. She wanted me to keep learning and found a school for me. I was glad I could go to school again. Sitting at home all day only makes you obsess about things.

## Not Scared Anymore

Right after I left home I missed my mother a whole lot. She asked if I was coming back. That was impossible. I felt bad for her because it wasn't her fault.

Now I go see my parents every other week. To my father I only say "Hi" or "Hello," nothing more. I'm not scared of him anymore, but I can't forget what happened. I get along with my mother better all the time. Except we never talk about the way things were before.

Some time ago I went with my sisters to a cousin's wedding. That was fun, buying clothes together and going to the hairdresser. The wedding was weird, though. There were uncles and aunts there I hadn't seen since I'd left home. "How grown-up you are," they said.

Sometimes I run into friends from my old neighborhood. Some of them are fooling around with weapons or drugs. One girl I know runs drugs for dealers. Kind of dumb. When I see that, I think to myself: I didn't get dragged down into that. Why not? I don't know. I get along well with people, make friends easily. They help me along. But in the end, you still have to do it by yourself. You're the one who decides to go look for help, to keep learning, whether you want to see your parents again. You decide for yourself.

## A Star

For six months I've had my own apartment, sharing it with another girl. I'm enjoying it here. My future's in the restaurant business. It's a great profession—totally, if it works out. And people have confidence in me. The restaurant I apprenticed at last year got a star. My work was only a part of it, but I'm proud anyway. You don't get a star just like that. Absolutely everything's got to be perfect. I go out on weekends. I like being with all kinds of people. People with really different ideas. Book nerds, party animals, gay guys, it doesn't make any difference to me. Those megaparties, I think they're awesome. Keep partying till early in the morning. Alcohol or pills? Don't need them. I just keep on keeping on.

# Don't Touch Me

My name is Sietse and I come from Sri Lanka. My parents adopted me when I was a couple of months old. It wasn't because they couldn't have children of their own. They just wanted to give children from the Third World a better life. I have a sister from Bangladesh, a brother from India, a sister from Haiti, and a Dutch foster sister from Zwolle.

## Birth Parents

My parents told me that my biological mother couldn't take care of me. She was much too young when she had me, about fourteen, I think. I don't have a picture of her but I imagine that she's small and has long hair. Nobody knows who my father is. I wasn't worried about this before. Now that I'm living in a youth home I think about it more. I'd like to visit my biological mother sometime, just to see who she is.

I think life's easier for children who grow up with their birth parents. It seems reassuring to me. I don't think I've had such a great life. Of course that's my own fault, but not just my own. My parents didn't really know what to do with me either. But I'm still grateful to them. If they hadn't adopted me, I probably wouldn't even be alive now.

## Afraid of Death

I've always been afraid of death. When I was twelve years old I got really sick. It started with my hand. It wouldn't work anymore, I kept dropping everything. I had a really bad feeling about it. I didn't dare tell my parents at first, but finally I went with my mother to see the doctor. They put me in the hospital the next day. It turned out to be exactly the illness I'd been afraid of. Funny, you think you've got something and then you've actually got it.

The first few days in the hospital I didn't sleep. I thought I was dying. I was super thin and the other kids in the ward looked awful too. My father was with me all the time, he slept beside me. I cried a lot because of the pain. The worst thing was the punctures. Do you know what a bone marrow puncture is? It's done with a really big needle, the doctor pushes on it with all of his weight and then you feel it rip. It goes straight through your bone.

After a year I was cured. I never told anybody I had

that illness. Not here at the youth home either. I'm scared they'll raze me about that when we fight and stuff. And if that happens, I'll really lose it.

## Don't Touch Me

When I was lying there in the hospital, I prayed every day that I wouldn't die. I promised God all kinds of things: that I'd always believe in him and that I'd be good to everybody. But after you get better, you don't think about that anymore. At elementary school I was still a nice kid, but when I started at a vocational junior high, that all changed. I always had something to say. The teachers had to do only one thing wrong and I'd fly off the handle. People should never grab hold of me, then I get totally dangerous. I don't know why, but I can't stand it when people touch me. My parents know that. For example, if I go to camp, they'll warn the directors, "If you get into an argument with him, whatever you do, don't touch him."

I didn't just have fights at school, I had them at home with my parents too. At first they were about little things: being late, not listening, messing around with motorbikes. Homework was another sore point. I wasn't a whiz, but my parents thought I should try harder to do my best. After a while the fights got worse and ended up getting physical.

## Detached

As a kid I was always very attached to my mother, I loved

her. But when I was thirteen, I didn't want to be that way anymore. I worried about her too much. Sometimes I'd go off on her and she'd have heart trouble. Then I'd be scared she was going to die. I didn't want to deal with it anymore, I didn't want any downers. That's when I detached. I had to distance myself, be free of my mother.

OK, how do you detach? At night when you go upstairs, no good-night kiss, no hugging, and if you're having a problem with something, no going to your mother. That's what you have to do. It worked, too. All in all, I didn't cry for a year.

My parents say this is one of the reasons I had to go to the youth home. At first I thought it was a bad idea, but finally I agreed. It was better for us, for my parents and for me.

## All Together

Because of the youth home I got to know a group of boys. They were really a kind of gang. These boys were dark-skinned too. If you're with them, you don't have to be scared of anything. In fights in the city, you all go for it together. You help each other, you care a lot about each other.

We had fights with Turks a lot. There's something about them I don't like. But I'm down on racist skinheads the most. They come up to you and act tough, showing you their shaved heads and Dutch flags. And then they start shouting, "What are all you black people doing here? Go back to your own country!" Well, I've got Dutch parents, but if your parents aren't white, you feel totally dissed. If I think back on that group now, it puts my head in a total spin. We had knives and guns that we used to threaten people or rob them. You try to make a good rep for yourself in the city. Well, a bad rep, really. Everybody moves out of the way for you, you've got power. Some girls really want to be your woman because of that.

But I didn't sleep well if we'd threatened other boys. You're scared yourself sometimes, and if you know how something feels, you don't want them to go through it.

## Not Coming Back

After a year I was transferred to another youth home. To be honest, I was relieved. Those days were a drag. It seems like you're all that and everybody's scared of you. But it's better just to talk to somebody, like now. That's a lot more fun.

Sometimes I see people looking at me, they can be thinking all kinds of things about you. That's why I try to present myself as well as possible. Like with my girl-friend's parents: I introduced myself very politely.

Now I can get along better with my own parents. I don't become aggressive as quickly. But the relationship isn't like it used to be. I do care about them, but in a different way. That sense of attachment won't come back.

*Sietse was taken out of the youth home two months after this conversation and went to work for a farmer in France in the Learning Experience Project.*

# My Own Life

## BRENDA

**18, lives with her boyfriend and daughter**

One thing's for sure: things will turn out all right for me and for my daughter too. Naomi's future looks rosy. She'll never have the life I had. I'll make sure of that.

## Everything Closed

I'm a Christmas baby, the oldest of five. When I was little, my parents were real parents, but when they became addicted, all that changed.

What I still remember well were those hot summer days at home. I was about ten. Everything was closed. Windows, curtains, and we had to stay inside. The kids on the block went to the pool. We couldn't go because there wasn't any money. I knew where it was all going: for liquor and drugs. But if my parents were in a bad mood like that, it was best not to say anything. It might take a long time or a short time, but they always got into an ugly fight. The neighbor lady would come get us and we'd stay with her until we were called.

## Asking for Money

The older I got, the more I had to take care of my little brother and sisters. I got them up, made sure they went off to school and did their homework. I think I was a kind of mother to them. When I was fifteen, they were taken out of our home. I was really, really angry. I had the feeling they were being taken away from me. My parents were also upset about it. But on the other hand, they were relieved. When my father was sober and my mother "straight," they realized they'd done wrong, that we weren't living a normal life.

There were times that there wasn't enough to eat. Then we'd have to make do with a slice of bread and peanut butter. Usually I was sent out to get money. I'd have to go to the parents of girls I knew with a note. Sometimes these people would get mad and blow up at me. I thought that was so horrible. After all, I couldn't do anything about it, could I? If I refused to go they'd send my sister. In those days I could think of only one thing: when will this be over?

## My Own Life

Actually, I'm living the kind of life I always wanted: a steady boyfriend, living together, getting diplomas, and a child. But I'm still living with my parents. They live on the street behind ours, and if they're fighting, my mother comes and gets me to referee. My boyfriend says I should create more distance and live my own life. But they're my parents, after all. I don't think I love them, but I do care about them.

Earlier this week I heard an ambulance in their street. I went over right away to see if something had happened to my mother. I'm always afraid it's going to end badly, that my father's going to do something to my mother. Once my father's drunk, he doesn't know what he's doing. My mother often says she's going to leave him. But she doesn't. They've been divorced three times and married three times.

## I Know What I Want

When my little brother and sisters were taken out of the house, I didn't have to go. I did get a social worker, but she thought I was too independent to go to a home. I was incredibly proud of that.

## Both Pregnant

When I was pregnant with Naomi, my mother was pregnant with my sister. I thought it was absurd. She couldn't even take care of her other children. What was she going to do with a baby? It was a strange situation. I was temporarily living with the neighbor lady. One morning I received a note saying my sister had been born. The note said what her name was and asked if I could give them fifty guilders. My sister had been born two weeks early, so they didn't have any diapers.

At first I didn't want to go, but the neighbor lady said, "Go on over. Your mother's trying to reach out to you." I went home and from that moment on we hit it off. My mother started caring for me like a real mother. My belly kept getting bigger and it bothered me. My mother would brew up some fennel tea and ask me if I wanted something to eat. Even my father noticed me and bought little things for his granddaughter. But a month before my due date, it was all over. My father was drinking again and my mother was calling her dealer to have a runner come by. Everything I'd gone through before with them started all over.

## Help

My boyfriend said I had to get out of there as quickly as possible. That's when I went to my social worker for help. Before, I needed nothing from her. I didn't trust people like that, because those same people had taken my sisters away. But my social worker never forced anything on me. She only said, "If you need anything, just come to the

office." And when I asked for help, she came through. She looked for a place for my boyfriend and me and the baby that was on the way.

## Much Too Nice

The day Naomi was born was the most beautiful day of my life. If I can take good care of her, I'll be happy. The first thing I do when money comes in is buy everything for Naomi. After paying rent and utilities, we have 125 guilders left to spend each week. Sometimes I get some money from my parents. I'm happy about that, but on the other hand: they come by every day. Usually they ask for chicken, because they know I always have some on hand. Sometimes they want money. If I have some, I give it to them. My boyfriend says I'm much too nice to everybody. But even if you were my sworn enemy, if you were in trouble, I'd help you. I know what it's like.

## Efteling Park

My younger brother and sisters now live in a home for children. On their free weekends they come stay with me and on their vacations they stay a week. I hope they have nicer lives now. I teach them that they have to take care of themselves first and then take care of others. My youngest sister, my parents' baby, is living with a foster family.

I'm not jealous of kids who had it better at home than

I did. But still, there were a lot of things we didn't have. Going to Efteling Park, Duinrell, Centre Parcs, every child talks about that. I still haven't ever been there. But my boyfriend says, "I'll let you see it all."

# On The Run

**LEYLA**

18, lives with a foster family

The day my father came out of jail was the most beautiful day of my life. I was twelve years old and hadn't seen him in eight years. Together with my family we picked him up and went home. My mother had prepared all his favorite foods. We were all very happy. I'll never be able to forget that day.

## Iran

I was born in Tehran, the capital of Iran. We lived on a busy street, in a big house. In Iran, life indoors is very different from life outdoors. At home you can do whatever you want, outside it's another world. There the government's the boss. Girls have to wear scarves on their heads out in the street and put on a long dark coat. We can't play certain sports and can only go into certain kinds of studies. I think those rules are strange, my parents do too. But the worst thing is that you can't talk without being scared.

I was still little when my father got picked up. They came to the house to take him. My father had burned forbidden papers and books, but they were still able to find a lot. I didn't understand why my father was gone. It had something to do with politics, but I didn't get it. I was scared and thought they'd come take me away too, but my mother said, "No, that won't happen. Just don't think about that."

## Older and Quieter

When I saw my father again after all those years, I was shocked. He was very different from how I remembered him, older and quieter. He was abused in the prison. His hand is paralyzed and his head bothers him. He's turned completely bald. I don't know what those people did to him.

In the beginning there was a lot to get used to. My father was an architect, but he couldn't work anymore. He was usually busy with books. I loved to sit near him. Other people may have thought he was stern, but he was very kind to me. Those were good times. In the summer we'd go north on vacation. It was nice and warm at the sea.

## Proposal

Then there was this man: he wanted to marry me. He

lived two streets down. I didn't know him, I'd never seen him before. The man was thirty-eight and had a wife. I was sixteen. He asked to marry me through a woman my mother knew. My mother and I actually thought it was really ridiculous. We had to laugh. I couldn't believe the man was serious. He works for those in power. At home we have another culture, we think very differently from him. He must have known that. We said no right away through my mother's friend. I thought that was the end of it, but it was just the beginning.

My younger brother, who was fifteen, was picked up. He was wearing a T-shirt with an American flag on it. He was questioned for a whole day by the committee. They beat him, too. We weren't surprised, because these things happen to other people as well. But the next day the man called up. He said, "That wasn't an accident. I know everything about your family, also about your father's past. There are other things I can do if you don't marry me."

## Kidnapped

After that day, other things happened. My father's car was set on fire. We went to the police, but it didn't help. They said, "That man works for the government. He protects the people. How can you have complaints about a man like that?"

I think the man's crazy, absolutely crazy. People don't do things like that, I still can't believe they would. They

kidnapped me four times. I'd just get yanked off the street and into a car. They'd shove my head down and drive to a quiet place. Then they'd start questioning me: "What kind of work do you do? What organization do you work for? We know everything, but you have to say it yourself." I would start to cry and say I didn't work for any organizations, that I was simply taking an English course. In the evening, the man would call up with new threats.

## The Only Way

For as long as I can remember I've wanted to be a dentist. During vacations I'd always take extra courses to get my diploma sooner. The summer I turned seventeen, I took the university entrance exams. I passed and went to get my acceptance card. When I got there, my card had disappeared. They said that I had no permission to study because my parents were politically active.

I was sick with grief and didn't go outside anymore. One morning I tried to commit suicide. With pills. My younger brother found me. At first I was happy I was still alive, but not later on. My parents decided I had to leave the country. My father said, "This is the only way. You have to show me how strong you are. We love you, you have to make your future." I didn't want to go, I wanted to stay with my parents. If they have problems, then so do I. But my mother said, "I know these people well, I know what they're capable of. You're still young, you still have a life to live."

### Escape

With my uncle I left for Turkey. We had to pay $6,000 to arrange my escape. After ten days, my uncle put me on a plane to the Netherlands. At Schiphol Airport I got through customs no problem: I had a fake passport. Outside, somebody would be ready to help me. But the woman said I had to go to the police, and walked away. I didn't know what to do and was very scared. I asked for directions to the police station but didn't dare go in. A policeman saw me crying and asked what was wrong. I said, "I escaped," and began to cry again.

### Dream

I've been living in the Netherlands for ten months now. First I was in a refugee center, then I was placed with a foster family. They're sweet people. I really wanted to live in a family. If I'm by myself, I think about Iran all the time.

My big dream is that my family can come here. But first I need to get a residence permit. I've already been turned down twice. There's still a chance that I can get a scholarship to study dentistry. That'll maybe help a little. My lawyer doesn't believe in it, but I went to talk with the refugee agency for students myself and was invited for a second interview. Nobody can say what happened better than I.

### Missing

Since I've been in the Netherlands I've talked to my

mother on the phone three times. Last Sunday she called from a secret number. She said everything was going well, but I was worried about my father. Then my mother told me my father was missing. I don't know for how long already, she didn't want to say. I'm afraid my father was picked up because I fled the country. I told my mother, "Then I'm coming back. If somebody has to die, it should be me. My brother still has a right to a father, I know what it's like to miss your father." My mother started to cry. She said I had to stay. She's writing me a letter in which she'll tell me everything.

# Keep On Being Nice

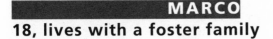

**MARCO**

**18, lives with a foster family**

If people ask me about my real parents, I say I don't have any. They do exist, but I'd rather not be reminded of them. What's happened, you can't rewind. I'd rather look ahead.

I'm proud of what I've achieved. First I went to a remedial school, then after that to a special ed high school. It's really just like a normal school, but they don't go as fast. I can't learn so well, that's because of the problems at home, I think. But now I've got a steady job.

## Always Cheerful

I'm a driver's assistant for a soft-drink wholesaler. Last week my boss offered me a contract. He thought I was

that good. He said I'm always cheerful and never come to work in a bad mood.

In the mornings we set out the orders. Then we load the van and are on our way. In the afternoons we usually make a second delivery. I think it's an incredibly fun job.

In five years my life will look like this: I'll have my driver's license, a small house, and a wife. She'll have to be nice, sweet, and normal. It doesn't matter to me if she's smart and pretty or not. The most important thing is that you have to make do with her your whole life, right? That you don't get divorced. And I hope I'll be happy then. I'm happy now too, even though I don't see any members of my family.

## All Split Up

I lived with my parents until I was six. I thought it was nice living together. My mother was always cheerful. My father worked and I thought it was nice when he came home. There were problems, but I didn't know that. Later, when I'd heard everything I thought: was it really so nice living together?

One day I was at the house of friends with my youngest sister. My mother and oldest sister came over, crying. They said, "The children have to leave the house." People had come to take us away. We got into a car and drove off. My parents didn't come along. I thought we were being kidnapped. My mother broke down and cried, I remember that. My father looked angry and surprised.

I have six brothers and sisters. We all got split up. Most of them I never saw again after that day. I don't know how they're doing now. Are they married? Do they have children? Are they dead? I'll never know. That'll keep being a bad feeling my whole life.

It's incredibly fun to be in touch with one brother. I don't see him very often. If I see him once a year, I'd call it lucky. He has a very busy job in the clothing industry. He did get a little higher up than I did. We never talk about before. My brother says he's busy with his own life now. And that's what I'm doing too.

## Deceived

From when I was six to when I was eleven I lived in a children's home. I saw my parents once or twice a month. First they came to visit, later we arranged to meet in a mall. But since I've known what happened, I never want to see them again. Either of them.

I was deceived by my parents. They knew the truth, but I had to hear it from somebody else. My father sexually abused my sisters. My mother was his accomplice. She knew about it but did nothing to stop it. My social worker told me that I was treated like trash. I was beaten and stuck in a closet. That was the reason we were taken away from home.

At first I didn't want to believe it. I thought my parents were nice. But then I started thinking and said: sure, it could have happened. I remember a couple of things. Once I was thrown against a chair. I had a gash in my head. And I still remember we were never allowed to go into our father and mother's room.

## A Kind of Family

From the children's home I went into a group home. That's very different. You wake up in the morning and breakfast and everything's all ready. There are fewer children there and the house parents stay with you twenty-four hours a day. They don't switch. It's really a kind of family. With my first house parents, I liked things a lot. After three years they stopped doing it because they had problems with the agency. Another boy and I stayed on in the house and other house parents came.

In the beginning it wasn't much fun. They changed everything in our house, the curtains, the carpeting, and the living room. There was one advantage, though: they had a dog. The first day when they let him out of the car he immediately came running up to us.

Now I get along very well with my house parents. Whatever I've achieved is also because of them. A couple of years ago things almost went wrong. I started stealing money from my house mother. At school I'd let other kids see how much money I had. Everybody could get candy and food from me. My house parents figured it out, but I said somebody else had done it. I think that's really awful. I especially hate lies. If you live together in a house, you have to trust each other. Every time I lied, I'd cry. Generally I don't cry a lot. I only cry if I have to.

## No Excuse

It's pretty hard living without your own parents. My mother really wanted to keep seeing me. But she knew what had happened at home and hadn't done anything to help my sisters. I thought she was a coward, really. Later I thought that maybe she didn't dare do anything. My brother helped my mother with a divorce later. But she didn't want to go through with it. She still chose to be with my father.

## Keep On Being Nice

My house parents have taken the other boys to the little summer house in France. It's fun being together there, you know. We can really party with each other. And I've got a lot of friends there, more than here. I think it's too bad I can't go along. France is the greatest thing there is. But, well, work comes first.

The hardest thing about my work is the customers. Sometimes you're labeled because of stuff that has nothing to do with your job. But you have to hold your-self back, you can't get angry. You have to keep on being nice while they're being cranky.

# Last Chance

RON

**17, lives with a foster family**

Coke wasn't really the thing. Pills, that's what I thought was really awesome, that was more for me. You talk really well, you become open and honest. I've smoked some dope, too, but that's more for foreign guys. House-party kids tend to use crank.

If I had kids and I noticed that they were doing drugs, I'd really set them straight. I wouldn't hit them, but I'd tell them what I'd gone through and seen so that they'd really be scared.

## A Mess

At our house it was a mess. My father's been drinking for as long as I can remember. When I was little, it didn't bother me. I was allowed to do a lot for my age. My mother had to laugh when I told her what I'd been up to. She was very lenient. And when my father was drunk, he thought everything was fine. Then I wouldn't even have to go to school.

I did realize that things were getting worse and worse between my parents. They were always fighting. When I was twelve, they divorced. My little brother and sister and I stayed with my mother. But she was being treated by a psychiatrist and couldn't cope alone. Every week she'd go find my father. A year after the divorce they got married again. I thought that was weird. But after six months my father left for the second time.

## Ecstasy

From that time on, I went my own way. My mother took heavy tranquilizers and got even more out of it than before. She thought everything was OK. I don't know how many schools I went to at that time. I skipped a lot. I'd go for a week and skip for three. I'd hang at the house all day with friends, playing music and watching TV or videos. And my mother just wrote notes to the school. Not just for me but for my friends, too.

I was thirteen when I started with Ecstasy. I'd rip off tranquilizers from my mother. I tried them with a friend. And I went on from there. I got to know more and more people who did or dealt drugs. At the same time, my mother started doing coke. It didn't interest me. My friends and pills were more important to me.

## She Didn't Care About Anything

Now and then my father would come by. He'd take a cab from The Hague to talk with my mother. But it always turned into a fight. I'd take my mother's side and would start to fight with my father. Because of those drugs I became stupid and aggressive.

At that time I placed all the blame on my father, but later I saw my mother's mistakes too. She didn't care about anything. If we fought, she'd give me pills so I'd keep my mouth shut. She went out every evening to some bar or other. During the day she'd lie in bed, at six o'clock she'd get up, put on her makeup, and leave. She didn't do any cooking anymore. Girls I knew cared for my younger brother and sister. At a certain point they went to live with my father. That was a good thing, too. They were getting smarter and smarter. My little sister started acting like somebody who's sixteen when she was only nine.

## Almost Destroyed

That period of time with my mother is the saddest time I can remember. I was fourteen and was on crank. My mother was addicted to coke and dealt at home. More and more friends came and went at the house. It was public knowledge: at Ron and his mother's it's awesome, you can just get high there. Sometimes there were twenty people there. I can still remember that New Year's I came home and the whole room was filled. Some guy says to me, "What're you doing here?" I said,

"I live here, asshole," and smashed the dude in the face. It turned into a huge fight.

Living that way goes nowhere. I really got sick of it. One time I was at a house party and had popped a lot of pills. I started coughing and blood came up. In the hospital it turned out that the walls of my stomach were almost destroyed.

There was one person who helped me then. That was my girlfriend. With her, I could talk. I started thinking about whether this was the life I wanted to live.

## Kicked Out of the House

My mother and I kept getting crazier. We started physically attacking each other over money and drugs. Not long after New Year's we were kicked out of the house by the police. It was one big mess: the furniture was busted, the walls were covered with graffiti, and the radiators had been removed.

My mother went to her parents. I was out on the street. My girlfriend convinced me at that point to go to the youth home.

When I got there, I wanted to leave again right away. Imagine: you're sitting there with all these guys in the middle of the woods. I was placed in a family group. The first few days I didn't say anything. Not to the guys, not to the group parents. I thought they were idiots, but that's what I thought about everybody.

I lived with those people for almost two years. I developed a good relationship with them. They helped me a lot. I didn't do crank anymore and went to school as usual. We also took vacations in Germany, France, and Belgium. I thought that was awesome. I'd never been out of the country before.

But when I was in the program for independent living, things went wrong. In no time at all the guys from the youth home were smoking Indo at my place. It got to be just like it had been at home. I had to leave the youth homes program and was advised to live somewhere with a family atmosphere. But I didn't have a family. The program administrator said to me, "There may be one place you can go, but it will be your last chance."

## Liking This Better

The people I'm living with now actually have a kind of deluxe foster family. Three of their own children, three foster children, two young mothers with babies, a little boy from the youth home, and I live there. At supper there are fourteen people at the table.

The atmosphere is really good, different from the group home. Here they believe in evangelism. At first it didn't really interest me, but that's changed. A couple of times I went along to Praise evenings and an Awakening. That's when people get together to worship God and sing. At first I thought it was strange, but one time I myself was touched by the Holy Spirit. It was like this: a man talked about something in a sermon and it was all about me, about my childhood. He also talked about forgiving. That touched me.

A lot of things happened that I think are miracles. Now I can say no to drugs. And I got my diploma even though I didn't have any chance to anymore. Last week was the award ceremony. I'm totally proud. Nobody thought I'd make it. My friends may call me crazy now because I believe in God. But I like this better.

# Not A Conventional Life

**MAARTEN**
**16, lives in a transition home**

This week I'm having a party. I passed my secondary school exams. And do you know what the best part of it is? My diploma says "Maarten." Actually, that's not my name, in my passport I have a Moroccan name. I found that out some time ago. But everybody calls me Maarten, I don't need a Moroccan name. I've already been busy for months to have it officially changed. Government workers, well, you know how that goes. If it keeps going like this, I'll have to go to the prime minister.

## A Real Family

My father was born in Morocco. He comes from a very big family and grew up in a foster family. When he was fifteen, he left. He lied about his age and applied for a passport under his foster family's name. So my last name isn't really real either.

My father traveled through Spain, Portugal, France, and Belgium. Finally he found work in the Netherlands and met my mother here. I grew up together with four brothers and sisters near a big city.

We haven't lived together for five years now. I do miss it. I'd rather live as a real family. But I don't know how things would have turned out if they had kept going the way they were. My father was an alcoholic and gambled. My mother tried to hide this. She wanted to protect us but was able to do less and less against it. She wasn't ever cheerful anymore and looked different, very pale. She also started getting sloppy. When I was eleven, my mother entered a psychiatric hospital. She was very depressed. A year later, when she left the hospital, my parents divorced.

## An Empty House

At first I didn't want to believe my parents were getting divorced. Sometimes you heard something on TV and my Vietnamese friends' parents had split up too. But I never thought something like that would happen to me. I'd only seen my father drunk a couple of times. In the morning at breakfast he was always cheerful. He'd sing songs with us. If my mother had told me sooner what was going on, I might have been able to do something about it.

I was left alone with my father and sisters. My oldest brother had already left the house and my youngest brother went to live with an aunt. So it was a very empty house. One night I heard my father coming home drunk. He went to my sister's room and stayed with her a very long time. I don't know what happened. My sister left the house in the middle of the night and my father destroyed everything in her room.

The next day my mother came over. She had come to take us away from my father, but I didn't realize this. I wanted to go to Youthland, that's a retreat for children. My mother brought me there. At Youthland I told a boy who was a total stranger about everything that had happened. Funny, isn't it, I never saw that boy again.

## The Other Side of the Country

Since I was twelve years old I've lived in six different places. First I went with my sister to live with my grandfather and grandmother, all the way on the other side of the country. It was boring. My grandparents sit in front of the television all day. Their favorite thing to watch is the news. At first I didn't know anybody, which made it even more boring. Luckily I met Niels at school. We were both standing alone in the school yard and then we ended up together in the same class. That's how we became friends.

After a year I went to a foster family my grandfather and grandmother knew through the church. It seemed like a fun idea to me. Besides, you can't spend your entire life with your Granny and Gramps, can you?

## That Tiny Yard

I don't like to remember my foster family. They lived with their two children in one of those manicured new developments with a yard. They were so proud of that tiny yard of theirs. At first they were being way too nice, but I don't appreciate it when other people try to be your parents. I already have a father and a mother. They thought my father was a really strange man. Well, he thought they were strange too.

They had really weird rules and I kept forgetting them. Then they'd get angry. If anything happened at their house, if for example some food had been snitched, I usually got the blame. Their own daughter could do no wrong. Their real child came first, their adopted child second—because they'd had the kid for a long time already—and I came last. I went away as often as possible. Usually I was at Niels's. Wherever Niels went, so did I. After nine months I left that foster family.

## By Some Book

I often felt lonely. Every time you go to another place you're all on your own again. After a year and a half at a youth home, I lived in a group home for ten months. But I didn't feel at home there either. They did everything by some book and made this whole system. Each kid got a

color: I was black. That means a black towel, black washcloth, black waste basket, black sheets, and a black cup in the kitchen cupboard. You were only allowed to use the stuff with your own color on it. The place was depressing. I have a problem with people wanting to lay down all the rules for you. To avoid any arguments, I usually went to my room. The group parents didn't like that. One day they said, "We think it would be wise if you left."

Now I've been living for some time in a transition home again. That's to prepare you for the independent living program. There are rules: you have to be home before twelve o'clock and report where you're going, but you can live with that. At least there isn't somebody who's watching every little thing you do.

## Not a Conventional Life

I still see my family regularly. My mother lives nearby. She's kind of married to a woman. Sometimes she's a little better, but she's depressed a lot. My father got married again to a real Moroccan woman. He's seriously working on his faith and isn't drinking anymore. If I want to, I can go live with him. But I don't like the atmosphere there. My father lies there asleep in the evening and this woman has to do everything. And I can't stand that irritating language of theirs, I don't understand a word.

What I like to do most is visit my brothers and sisters. My oldest brother is my role model. He doesn't have a real conventional life like most people. He has experienced a lot. He has lived in youth homes and on the street and been in jail. When I'm at his place, we listen to music together and play guitar.

## Growing

In September I'll be starting at a business college. I'd like to have my own business later. An office job isn't for me. I'm realistic. I hope I'll earn enough to pay my rent and eat well. I do have a wish, though: my one hope is that I'll still grow. I don't believe it will happen, but it might very well. Bones often start late, sometimes they can still suddenly keep on growing.

# Everything With My Feet

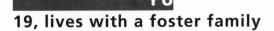

**YU**

**19, lives with a foster family**

Do you know why I'm disabled?
Just after I was born I got jaundice.
I was born in Peking.
I lived there for eleven months.
Then we went to the Netherlands.

My real parents didn't take very good care of me.
They worked in a restaurant.
We lived upstairs.
I always had to lie on the floor.
When I was six, I went to a home.
I cried every night.
In fact I was angry. Why hadn't they said anything?

## New Parents

When I went to school, I told the social worker,
"I think the home's a waste of time."
I didn't meet any people there.
I wanted a new dad and mom in a normal house.
I wanted to go away more, go on vacation.

I thought my new mom was awesome right away.
Because she could talk with me.
She taught me sign language, with my feet.

Sometimes I longed for my Chinese mother.
The first day, she came over.
It made me cry.
After that, never again.

I see my Chinese parents on birthdays.
We usually go see them.
Then I get cake with whipped cream frosting.
I don't think they understand me now.

## Everything with My Feet

I'm at the Bio-Mytyl school.
But I'm leaving.
I'm going to residence housing.
With my own room and kitchen.
But I have to wait first.
I want to be famous.

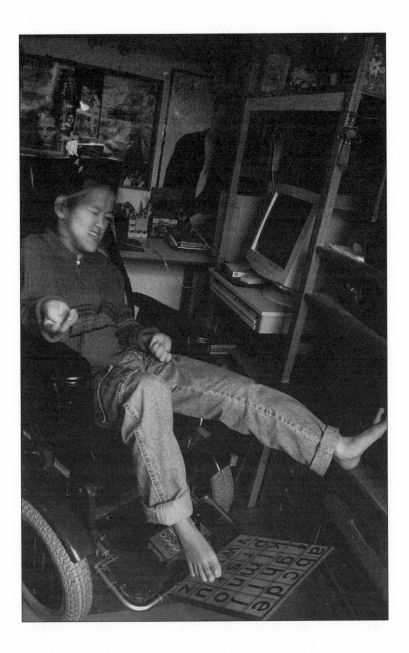

I'm proud I can do everything with my feet:
Talking, math, and writing letters.

## The Ideal Man
I want to get married.
He'll have to be strong.
And good-looking.
He'll have to know about wheelchairs.
He can't be disabled.
Because then he won't really be able to talk with me.
And he has to be able to carry me.

I don't want any children.
That's tough.
Because I'm disabled.
I can't feed them or take care of them.
I don't think that's too bad.

I'm in love with the bus driver.
Not very long, six months.
He's not in love with me.
I'm also a Henny Huisman fan.
He's funny.
I've gone to his studio.
And he wrote me a letter.

## The Most Important Thing
I'm proud that I'm Chinese.

I want to go to China sometime.
My grandma died there.
I miss her.
She took care of me.

Loneliness? I don't know what that is.
The most important thing in my life is:
I don't want to be disabled.
I think it's mean that I can't vote.
Other young people can learn or work.
I have to stay at home.

I'd rather walk.
Then I'd go to a concert.
To see the *Back Street Boys*.

I have the most problem eating.
I can't swallow.
People think I'm a baby.
I'm not a baby.
They should listen to disabled people.
But sometimes they have to get used to them first.

# I Could Do Anything

## ORAN

### 17, is in a reform school

The day I'm free, I'm going to stand outside this place first. Nice and quiet in the fresh air. Then my brother will drive up in his car. We'll drive to my mother's together. She'll have prepared a lot of food, Turkish food. I'll stay at home until evening, then I'll take a shower and go see my girlfriend. The next day I'll go to Turkey, to my father's grave.

## Little and Sneaky

You don't notice those kinds of things, but I do. I recognize them. When I see some of the kids on the street, I know they're doing wrong, that they might go in the wrong direction later.

In kindergarten I was little and sneaky. I saw all that

stuff in the classroom and took it home: scissors, glue, and felt-tips. At home I'd make little balls of glue and color them with the felt-tips. Nobody had a clue. Only later, in the fourth grade, they found out. A Parker pen had disappeared. The teacher, Miss Laura was her name, asked if I happened to know where that pen was. Well, I'd taken it home long before.

Still, I stayed through the last year at that school. After that I went to the junior high. And there you go: smoking cigarettes on the sly, Indo, I started drinking a little, stealing. The farther along I got the more I tried to get away with. Look, now I'm stuck here, but when I was on the outside, I didn't think of the consequences. Just like those kids on the street. You don't think about that until you're locked up.

## My Father and I

My father and I got along very well. I liked him and he liked me. He taught me to drive, I thought that was awesome. When I was fourteen he passed away. He'd been in the hospital for two months already. He had cancer. My mother hadn't told me anything until he got really ill. His legs were swollen with fluid. I saw one of the brown stripes from the radiation and then I knew enough.

I didn't go to visit him often in the hospital. Every time I went there he was a step closer to death. One Sunday evening I went for the last time, Monday it was finished, over, done with. I thought he was getting better, but suddenly the illness had spread.

## A Bus

When I was twelve or thirteen, the police were regularly at our apartment. About shoplifting, then about arson. My father worked and usually wasn't home. But one day I came in and my father was waiting for me. "What have you done?" he asked. I said nothing. But there was a letter from the police lying on the table. "What did you steal?" my father asked. He thought it was something small, another pen or something. But I'd stolen a bus, a tour bus. I'd driven it around. When people saw me, I left it at an intersection and ran out.

I had to appear in court and received a warning and a small fine because I had damaged the bus. I thought my father would be angry with me, but when we got home, he started to laugh: "I teach you how to drive a car and you go and steal a whole bus …"

## I Could Do Anything

I was quiet for a while, but after that I started up again. The awesome thing was you could do anything. Nobody said anything, they could never do anything to me. I had money for gambling, for smoking Indo, and for girls. I hung mostly with foreign guys. There aren't many Dutch guys who are into couples at that age. Dutch parents are different too, they ground you, for example. I used to

laugh at those guys when they had to stay home. Foreign parents spank their kids, that just makes you tougher.

My brother was on to me. He said to me, "Boy, you don't have to fool me. I was like that too, and you're in even deeper shit than I ever was."

When my father was lying in the hospital, I cracked a convenience store safe. I knew the man who worked there. He was a really good guy. It was a bitch, because he trusted me. But you don't stop to think, you're just busy looking for ways to do it.

When I got back from my father's funeral, the police were at the door. I had to appear before the judge for a third time. I got a hefty fine, a couple of days of community service working for a Halt Agency, and a compulsory course called Victim in Focus. The purpose of the course is that in ten hours you learn how it feels to be robbed, threatened, or beaten up. Well, I knew all about that. I've been robbed a couple of times too. I don't care. If your motorbike's gone, you steal another one, right?

## I Don't Know You, You Don't Know Me

Finally what put me here happened. I can't tell you what I did, but I was sentenced because of a very serious violent offense. The night after it happened, I called my brother. He came and got me and hid me away somewhere.

After a couple of days he said, "I'm bringing you to the police station, I'm going to turn you in. It's better for me and better for you. You'll see that later." I got angry and said he had to let me go. "I don't know you and you don't know me." But he didn't want that, and I knew why. My brother was just about to go to Turkey and I'd be staying behind all alone with what I'd done. It was a heavy offense, but the victim was still alive. They would find me and everything would start all over again.

That's why I went with my brother to the police. I had no idea what was in store for me.

I've been locked up for almost a year. It's my own fault. My parents didn't do anything. Upbringing plays a role, but nobody ever told me: there's your prey, go get it.

I hope I get out of here normal. I've already changed. Not too long ago I wouldn't have talked to you. I'd have thought: what does she want from me? I'm trying to be nicer, to think more positive thoughts. Look, you're here with a lot of guys and that produces certain kinds of tension. But if it looks like things are going to go wrong, I'll try to warn somebody first. I'll tell them they shouldn't come whining to me. Outside, I wouldn't explain anything, there it was just plain whale on them.

## Not for a Long Time
I'm trying to get a diploma here. Then at least I'll have

something. And after that I'm going to start saving so that I can buy my own business legally: a little café or restaurant. Sometimes I'm afraid things'll go wrong again. But you shouldn't think about that too much.

I have little contact with friends from before. Recently a guy called up. "When are you getting out?" he asked. That's right, when am I getting out ... Good question! Not for a long time.

# Family Is A Burden To Me

**FEYZULLAH**

**20, lives in a boarding house for young adults**

You know what I'm ashamed of? My nose. It looks like my father's nose, just as pointy. That's the worst, I think: I look more like my father than my mother, although I don't like my father. Luckily I'm not like him as a person. I'm not quick to get angry and I don't hit people. Certainly not my own family.

## Cherry Tree

I was born in Turkey, in a village close to a big city. I lived with my father, mother, and sister in an old house. My father was a farmer. He had a piece of land with his family where they grew wheat and corn. My mother liked gardening. She raised strawberries and plums and we had a cherry tree.

One day my father left for the Netherlands. When he came back, my parents argued. They separated and the court decided that my sister and I had to go with my father. That part happened very fast, I wasn't even able to say goodbye to my mother. I thought my father was happy with my mother. My feeling is that the divorce happened because of disagreements between my father's family and my mother's. That's the way it often goes in Turkey: families turn on each other.

## "Yengen"

Moving to the Netherlands was pretty scary to me. You go from a village to a city, in a totally different country with a different language, different children, and a different mentality. I was four and spoke only Turkish.

In the beginning the three of us lived together, but after a while my father remarried. This woman also came from Turkey and had never been outside the country. I called her "Yengen" at first, it means something like aunt. But my father said that I had to call her "mother." Which I did, or else I'd catch hell.

I thought my stepmother wasn't nice. My sister and I had to do all her work for her: wash dishes, make beds, shop for groceries. She was always over at the Turkish neighbors' gabbing. If she wasn't satisfied, she'd complain to my father that his son wasn't doing well.

Sometimes, together with my sister, I'd call my mother

in Turkey. I missed her terribly. She tried to give us support. "Keep it up just a little longer," she'd say.

## He Doesn't Like Us Anymore

When my half brother was born, it got worse. It seemed as if my father and stepmother loved only him. My father kept getting stricter with me. If I made even a little mistake, like spilling my food, he'd get angry. Then he'd start to shout and I'd get slapped. At first with his bare hand, but later he used objects. I got scared and avoided him as much as possible. At night in our room I'd talk with my sister. We both thought my father was slipping. My sister said, "My feeling is he doesn't like us anymore."

My father lives according to Turkish customs. He expects you to become a good Muslim and respect your family. Turkish parents who have been living here longer, for twenty years or so, are more modern. They seem more like Dutch parents. My father wants to live exactly like they did in the old days in Turkey. I never dared to stand up to him. Dutch boys are sometimes scared of their fathers, too, but they can always talk. I never had one normal conversation with my father.

Nobody knew how my father was at home. Whenever family came to visit, he was never physical. The only person I could tell was Batto, a friend from school. I'd go over to his house a lot. He happened to have very nice parents. When I saw them living like that and I saw my parents, I thought: this is impossible.

## Something Terrible

When I was fifteen years old, something terrible happened. I called my mother and got my aunt on the phone. She said, "Don't you know? Your mother was in a tractor accident and was killed on the spot." That had happened a week earlier! My father knew about it and my stepmother knew about it, but they hadn't told me for a whole week. My sister hadn't said anything either, because she was scared of causing me pain. When my father came home I yelled at him. I shouted "Bastard, dirty scum" at him in Turkish. It all came out, I just couldn't take it anymore. My father had never seen me like that, never before had I called him a bastard. He got angry. He didn't even think twice about the fact that I had lost my mother and that he should be comforting me. He started pounding on my back like crazy with a vacuum cleaner hose. I grabbed the hose away from him and ran out of the house.

## A Disgrace

Since that day I have never seen my father again. A cousin told me that my sister left six months after I did. My father wanted to marry her off to a Turkish acquaintance from our village who needed a residence permit in Holland. But my sister didn't want to, she loved another man. She ran away with her boyfriend and they've gotten engaged. My cousin thought it was a disgrace for my father and told me I had to find my sister. If she didn't want to marry the man the family had selected, I should shoot her. He'd take care of the gun. I told him, "You're crazy, like I'm going to kill my only sister!"

## Terribly Lonely

The day after tomorrow I'll turn twenty. In the four years I've been away from home, I've gone through a lot. After a youth shelter and a youth home I was in a transition home to go into the independent living program. I felt very lonely there. Sometimes I wouldn't talk to anybody for a whole weekend. After a couple of months a guy moved into the room next to mine and then things went wrong. I started smoking Indo and went to school less. I kept needing more money, so I went off to get it with this other guy. One evening we were caught breaking into cars. We were drunk and it wasn't until the next day that I realized what I'd done. I even had to stay locked up for a while. When I got out, I didn't know what to do. I'd been kicked out of school and had lost my spot for the independent living program. There was nowhere for me to go. The only person I had was my sister.

That's when I moved in with my sister and brother-in-law for a time. I slowly stopped smoking Indo there. My old school friend, Batto, came to see me and suggested we train to become painters. I've already earned my first certificate and I'm on a two-year contract. I'm really proud of that. The best part of the work is the final result. That you can completely fix up something that looks awful.

Right now we're working on a harbor crane. You work 120 feet above the ground. If you have a fear of heights, you can forget it, but I've never had that.

## Lost Two Children

I don't think my father knows how I'm living. He was angry that I left, because it's a disgrace for him if the family hears about it. But they have nothing to do with our family life. I have a problem with all that gossiping and turning against others. Family is a burden to me. Except for my sister, of course. I doubt my father's happy. He has lost two children. He must feel that, because it's his own blood. My sister and brother-in-law are expecting a baby in two months. If my father had done things differently, he would have been able to get to know his future grandchild.

# I'm
# Just
# Normal

**14, lives with a foster family**

I saw my mother for the last time when I was seven years old. I don't think of that every day, but I'd like very much to meet her. One day she'll suddenly be dead and I won't ever have talked with her. The idea of visiting her seems strange to me. I'm sure it doesn't happen like it does on television. Maybe she'd slam the door in my face. But she might also let me in and be very warm.

## Bad Reports

I'm almost fifteen and I've never lived with my parents. I can't picture anything. I'm used to living with foster parents. In the family I'm living with now I've stayed two years already and the plan is that I'll stay here. At first the foster care people didn't want to grant permission for this. They think I'm a difficult kid because they've had bad reports about me. I'm not supposed to fit into a family because I've been moved around a lot.

I know very little about the first years of my life. The only thing I have is my photo album. When I was born, my mother lived by herself. She never married my father. There are five other children from different fathers, but I only know my half sister. I grew up with her. My mother couldn't take care of us, so she put us into a children's home. I don't think I liked it, because I'm crying in every photograph.

After the children's home my sister and I spent four years in a group home. The photos from those days are a lot more cheerful. But the house parents quit, so we had to go somewhere else. Then we were placed with a foster family. I lived there until I was thirteen.

## No Photo

I don't have a single picture of that foster family. There are photos, but I don't have any. I left on bad terms and my foster mother says she sent my stuff to Poland in bags.

When my sister and I joined this foster family, it all seemed nice and fun: a real family with three children of their own. We had stayed overnight there a couple of times before. My foster parents said that they thought we were enjoyable children and called up to say they wanted us. We got presents and they had decorated a beautiful room for us. But pretty soon things went wrong. They expected

too much of us. If we did just one thing wrong, my foster mother would get snippy. Typically, foster parents have to take a training course, but they didn't think that was necessary. They were too proud to ask for help. My foster mother was very strict. I wet the bed, I couldn't help it. But she kept getting angry and hit me with the rug beater. When I woke up at night because my bed was wet, I wouldn't dare say anything and would crawl in bed with my sister.

## Incredibly Sick to My Stomach

I didn't know what I was supposed to do. I had a social worker, but what can you tell a man like that? He came to visit once every two months. He'd ask, "Well, Samantha, how are you?" And I'd say, "All right." I didn't want to say things were going well, but with my foster parents there I didn't dare to say things were going badly either.

The tension at the house grew. My foster mother felt we needed to eat more. For lunch we'd each get two sandwiches. That would make me incredibly sick to my stomach, my sister too. One time she spat the food out and then she had to eat it again. My foster mother just shoved it into her mouth. Down in the living room it got quieter and quieter. One day my sister came home and my foster father said, "Your bag is packed." My sister didn't have a clue, but she had to leave the house. When my sister was gone, the problems started with me. I was also forced to eat everything, even if I got so sick to my stomach I had to throw up.

## Slept in a Hollow

A couple of days before my thirteenth birthday I ran away. I couldn't take it anymore. I had gone to the beach with a friend that day. I wasn't allowed to hang around with her, that was some new rule. My foster mother had seen us and I had to go straight to my room and write lines for punishment. It had never occurred to me before, but I got so angry that I ran away that evening. That night I slept in a hollow, in the bushes where we always played.

The next day I walked to my friend's and the police were there. I wasn't upset, I wanted to be found so that my foster parents would know I was very angry. The police were nice, they understood the situation right away. I did have to go back to my foster parents' because it was a weekend. The police told me it would be better not to talk to my foster mother. Of course there was a bad atmosphere in the house. It wasn't until Monday that my social worker came. He took me aside and said, "Your foster parents want you out, today." I wanted to say goodbye to my foster mother, but my foster father said I should get into the car right away.

I never saw them again after that. I still think about them. My foster mother could be really awful, but there were also times when she was very kind to me.

## Everybody Knows Everybody

The foster family I live with now is very different. They had foster children in their home before and they can deal with it. They have four children of their own. Usually I feel really at home here, but sometimes I think: so is this it? They are Christian and I wasn't brought up that way. Faith is very important to them. I believe too, but when I look deeply, I have doubts. I can't picture it all. Sometimes I feel guilty that I work too little on my faith. What if you're in an accident, it isn't right to start praying at the last minute, is it?

Since I've been living here I go to church every Sunday. I often think it's boring, but staying at home alone isn't a lot of fun either. Soon I'll be in catechism. At first I didn't want to, but I know my foster parents would think it a shame if I couldn't be confirmed. I'm not looking forward to it. I'm scared it'll be just the same as the church choir: all these little groups in it, friends and family. Everybody knows everybody else and I feel like a stranger among them.

Do you know where I feel most at home? At school. I feel they're the same as I am. One of my best friends is in my class. I can tell her everything. She knows I'm a foster child. I don't confide in everybody. Some kids don't even know what foster care is and start thinking weird things about you. But I'm just normal, just like other people.

## Total Trust

There are a lot of people I love: my sister, my friends, and my foster family. My foster parents say that they love me too. Still, I'm scared sometimes that it'll go wrong. I'm different from their own children. Maybe someday my foster parents will tell me I have to go. Maybe I'll want to leave sometime. But if they said that, I think I'd never totally trust anybody again.

I can't say I love my mother, because I don't know her. My sister is mad at my mother for what she did to us. I'm not mad: my mother couldn't take care of us, but she never abused us. And I heard she had a rough childhood herself, and then it's a little different.

# Fighting For Your Life

**JOEY**
**16, lives in a youth home**

I was a triplet, but my two brothers died. We were born three months early. I was only twelve inches long and weighed two pounds. My heart and lungs weren't well developed and I was completely transparent. My mother held me for twenty seconds and then I had to go to the children's hospital.

## Out of the Window

I only really got to know my parents when I was fourteen. They told me what the first years of my life were like. My mother was seventeen when she had me. She was addicted to drugs and did them during her pregnancy. That's why I was born early. After nine months I got out of the hospital. My parents were separated right after I was born, but they were still living in one house. They fought every day. My father decided everything for my mother: what clothes she was to wear, how she had to do her hair, and how she should present herself to the outside world. During the day he locked her up in the house so she couldn't go anywhere. She was a very beautiful woman and my father didn't want her to have any opportunities with other men. But one day my mother lowered the stroller out the window and then climbed out herself.

## Little Joey

My mother didn't have a house and drifted around with me. We lived everywhere: with friends, in abandoned buildings, and even on the street. Because of all those things, my social skills never developed. I was always crying and fighting, and I never listened. My mother couldn't take it anymore. When I was three, she dropped me off at my father's. He said, "I'll take care of little Joey." But he had no time and brought me over to friends. Through them I ended up in a children's home. That's when my parents lost me.

I spent four years in that children's home. It sucked. I always played by myself, outside on the street. I didn't like anybody. I only liked myself. When I was seven, I got foster parents. The administrator said to me, "Here is a mother for you, and a father." Well, I didn't even know what that was, a father and a mother.

## Out of Anger

My foster parents were old people. I don't know why they took me. Their own children and their foster daughters were already grownup.

I was a real handful for them. I didn't talk to them, only if I wanted to know something. I went ballistic a lot. My foster mother would sit on top of me. She was very fat and I couldn't get her off me. Then I'd pull my hair out of my head and bite my hands. Out of sheer anger, because I couldn't stand her being stronger. At a certain point I'd lie still and look at the ceiling. Then it would be over and she'd go away.

During that time I also saw a number of psychiatrists. They made me arrange furniture in dollhouses, do jigsaw puzzles, and finish stories. I always behaved myself with them and never threw a fit, because I knew that would put me at a disadvantage. Very hypocritical.

## You Don't Do Things Like That

Things really got out of hand at my foster parents' house. Naturally you feel you don't belong there. At school I didn't have any friends either. I didn't think those kids were on my wavelength, they were all so happy, playing their little games. I went my own way and didn't pay attention to anybody else. Sometimes I'd ride my bike into the city and stay away all night. I never told my foster parents what I was doing and they asked less and less. Maybe I was attached to them, but I was the one who decided how strong the tie was. At one point I stole a lot of money from them and had to leave. I was twelve years old then.

After a year in a children's home I was placed in this youth home. In my group there was a boy who became my friend. We're still best buddies now.

At night we'd go to each other's rooms to do drugs. Especially Indo and crank, but we also smoked heroin. We ripped stuff off from other boys to get money. We were "the Dynamic Duo." Looking back, I think: you don't do things like that, ripping off your group. But you do it anyway, because you're thinking only of yourself. That's the way it is with drugs.

## Two Big Kisses

As you get older, you want to know who your parents are. The first time I saw my father again, I was eight years old. My social worker had arranged a meeting. I sat and waited with my foster parents. Then my father came in and he gave me two big kisses on my mouth. I thought that was really weird, because he was a total stranger. He gave me my birth certificate, which he'd kept for me. I said almost nothing and after half an hour it was over. The next day I'd forgotten all about it.

Now I think the contact I have with my parents is very important. They tell me honestly about their lives. I recognize a lot of things about myself. That I go my own way, just like my mother, for instance. I also understand better why I was always so mad. I think I wanted to fight for myself, let others know I existed.

## Just Bad Luck

I have a lot of admiration for my father. He used to be part of the drug scene, but he got out of that. Now he's a conventional man, very proper and self-disciplined. I myself stopped doing drugs a couple of months ago, I think because I saw how my mother lives. She still isn't ever sober. She doesn't dare quit. I just forced myself. With me it's like this: I try for something and make sure I get it.

When I look back on my life, I see one big mess. I'm not angry at my parents. I don't have the right. At fourteen I come into their lives and who am I to say anything about them? It's too bad that they didn't try to have a normal family, though. They just lived the way they did. My mother was seventeen when she had me. What do you really know about the world then? Nothing. My father was older, it's true, but he himself had been in homes as a kid. You can't point the finger of blame. I just had bad luck.

## Her Breath

Of course there are things I could have done differently, but I'm proud that I kept myself afloat. Everything I have is my own doing. My whole person—how I am—I can thank myself for. I've almost got my high school diploma.

Then I'll go into an independent living program. In a year I want to go live with my girlfriend. I'm absolutely blown away by her. She is incredibly beautiful, she could be a fashion model any day. We're always there for each other. She is pretty withdrawn, but not with me. I really like being with her. Everything is beautiful: the warmth of her body, her voice, her breath.

# A Tight Group

**LAURA, ALEXANDER,
JERRY, MELANY**
all 15, live in a youth home

*Melany:* Another move, other new friends, another new school: those were my first thoughts when I heard that I was going to go to this youth home. But then, it was a choice between that or another emergency shelter. And you can't stay long at those shelters, but here you can.

## Arrogant

*Laura:* It bothers me when somebody asks me right away the first day why I'm here. So I say, "It's none of your business. I'll talk about it sometime later." It also bugs me when somebody arrogant comes in and starts boasting about themselves or about their parents.

*Melany:* But sometimes somebody acts arrogant, to show they've got attitude. When I came here three weeks ago, I wasn't looking forward to it. You're just nervous, scared they won't like you. At first it seemed like nowhere, but then Laura joined this group. And I thought she was nice right away.

*Laura:* Yeah, we hit it off from the start. I thought it was awesome that you were in it, or I'd have been the only girl in the group.

*Melany:* We'll probably get to be best friends, right?

## Homesick for My Dog

*Melany:* At first I was homesick a lot. For my friends, for my school, and for my dog. OK, my mother too. For everybody, really, except my father. I don't have any contact with him anymore.

*Jerry:* I don't get homesick at all. It's better here than at home. I don't see my parents that much. They don't come on my birthday. Well, so they don't. I'm not going to lose sleep over it. I've got a thick skin.

*Alexander:* I've been living here for over a year now. Before this, I lived with a foster family for ten years. With my parents, as I call them, I was much freer than here. I had my own room, my own friends, and the soccer club. I may sound like a nerd, but that's really what I'd based my life on.

*Jerry:* I was supposed to go to a foster family too, but it didn't happen because I was too old.

*Melany:* A family or a foster family has chosen you. You feel at home there, like you're part of things somehow.

*Laura:* You feel that your parents really care about you.

*Alexander:* They're always there for you.

*Jerry:* Yeah, until you get booted out. They're just doing their job.

*Melany:* Of course the staff helps, but I couldn't build up a relationship with them. In order to do that you have to be able to trust somebody completely. If I say something to one of the staff, it'll immediately be discussed in group meeting and then they'll all know about it. That's not very cool, is it?

*Alexander:* You know what it is with the staff? They come here, do their work, and go home. But they forget what they've gone through with you. They don't think about your problems anymore. With foster parents it's different.

*Jerry:* Still, I get along fine with the staff. Some of them don't work here anymore, but I visited them a couple of times.

*Alexander:* I've never been over to somebody's house. One time I snuck a peek into the window of a woman staff member.

*Laura:* I think the worst thing are those substitutes. Every time you have to get used to somebody else.

*Jerry:* That's where I have an advantage. I'm in a family group cottage and that couple signed on for five years.

## Helping Out a Little Bit

*Laura:* Sometimes I'm bored to death. Then it's like I don't live here, like I'm visiting. At home I saw my friends every day, now I hardly ever see them anymore. That's no fun. I miss home a lot.

*Alexander:* Laura, stop complaining. I like being together here. The interaction between people is good. You just have to help each other out a little bit.

*Melany:* When I went to my new school, Alexander bicycled with me. He knew the way and explained to me what the best way was to go in because you couldn't even tell where the front entrance was. After that we smoked a cigarette in the schoolyard. That was pretty cool. But even though I've made friends here, I feel lonely a lot.

*Jerry:* I can help you not to feel lonely, you know.

*Melany:* I don't mean it that way. I mean, if I call my mother and she's going on about how I can't go home that weekend, then I feel really bad.

*Jerry:* Just slam down the receiver …

*Laura:* If I notice that Melany's being quiet, then I try to comfort her and ask her what's wrong.

*Melany:* I think that's awesome. You, I'll talk to.

*Jerry:* I'll never talk about anything, even if they give me ten million guilders. Never to the staff. They start dragging up your past. Then they say something like, "Yes, you used to act that way before too, and that has something to do with your parents …"

*Alexander:* Yeah, and what on earth does your childhood have to do with it?

## Totally in Love

*Laura:* You can't go out with anybody here in the home. But if I were totally in love with a boy from here, I'd go for him.

*Jerry:* It does happen, but it's not allowed. Because of our problems, I think.

*Melany:* I think it's a good rule. If two people are having a relationship, it creates a group within the group. I've had a relationship here, and during any discussion, I'd take this boy's side. The staff doesn't like it. But what I really think is ridiculous is when one of the staff has a thing for one of the kids. Kids who come here have a past and they're coming here for their future. Staff should keep their hands off.

## Teased

*Jerry:* Almost everybody I know knows that I live in a home. Here in the neighborhood they're friendly and say hello to you, and I say hello back.

*Alexander:* Sometimes I've been teased about it. At school they told me I was wearing weird clothes. I said, "They're not that bad. Where I live just isn't as nice as where you live." Then one of the boys said, "Is it my fault you live in a home?"

*Jerry:* He should've said that to me, I'd have taken care of him pretty quick.

*Melany:* You can punch somebody, but it doesn't really hurt. If you touch somebody on the inside, that really hurts. I'm awesome at that.

*Jerry:* I never really know what to say. The first thing that occurs to me is to land a good punch.

*Laura:* At my school they don't make a big deal of the fact that I live in a home. Boys in my class have said they'd stop by someday.

*Melany:* I told them at school that I live here. But they already knew. "It's kind of cool over there, I think," one girl said. "Yeah," I said. "It's really a pretty tight group."

*A month after this conversation, Melany had to move into another home.*

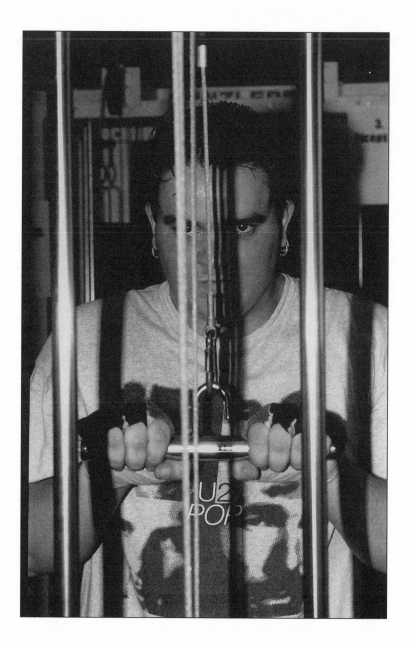

# Laugh When You're Scared

**SÉRGIO**

**16, lives in a youth home**

The name Sérgio hardly ever gets used here in the group. I'm known as Fats—that's my nickname. If friends call me that, I don't mind, but other people better not try. It bugs me anyway, people who judge me before they know me.

## Laugh When You're Scared

My first day at the youth home is something I won't easily forget: you get hazed. Usually they throw you in the creek, but in my case they crushed my breastbone. First I was kicked by a couple of guys and then some dude starts jumping up and down on my chest. I started to laugh and that guy thought I was laughing at him. But it just happens that I laugh when I'm scared. So he jumped super hard and "crack" went my breastbone. For a month I went around with it hurting. Now I'm one of the oldest in the group and pretty much get my way. Nobody dares to call me stupid for no reason.

## Absolutely the Worst

My mother comes from Angola, my father's from Mozambique, and I was born in Portugal. We lived with my brother and sister in a little village near Lisbon. We lived simply, but it was fun. School there started at two o'clock in the afternoon, so we could play outdoors all night. My father had a very good job, but he didn't know how to handle money. We didn't get much to eat. In Portugal I was also really skinny. Not that we were starving, but what we eat here in the Netherlands was, for us, a ten-star restaurant. Life in the Netherlands is a lot richer and lazier than in Portugal.

My parents didn't get along at all. One evening, I was four, they started arguing and my mother packed her bags. She left for the Netherlands with my uncle and aunt. I thought this was absolutely the worst. I woke up the next morning and my mother wasn't there. The only people I could cry with were my brother and sister. My father's somebody who has to "be tough."

Three years later my mother came to pick us up. I didn't recognize her at first, but she came running over to me and said, "Sérgio." I jumped into her arms and

she started to cry. Then I had to cry too, because if I see somebody crying, I start too.

## Illegal

The first place we stayed in the Netherlands lasted only four weeks. We were picked up by the police. It happened like this: I was at school and had a half-day Wednesday. My mother didn't know that. I got fed up with waiting and walked home by myself. I thought I knew the way. But all the streets looked the same and I got lost. Two men brought me to the police station. My mother was pretty mad at me. We were still illegal then and were immediately sent back to Portugal.

After a year my mother had saved enough to go to the Netherlands again with me and my brother and sister. She hoped to get ahead here, because the Netherlands is strong economically.

Soon we went to live with my stepfather. He's of Portuguese descent too, and is the father of my little sister. Right away our old clothes were thrown away and replaced by new ones.

On the weekends we'd all go out in his red Mercedes. I did get off on that. He was more of a father than my own father, he really helped us. But I thought it was no good. He was taking the place of my old father. That gives you a weird feeling: you don't know who your father is anymore.

## Smashed All the Windows

I wasn't really an easy kid. At school I used to hang with a group of older guys. We formed what we called a Posse. Jamie, a Dutch guy, was the boss. I wasn't afraid of him, but if you wanted to be with the Posse, you had to do what he told you. I've been picked up once or twice for shoplifting and one day I smashed all the windows at my school. Jamie and the other guys in the Posse thought I wouldn't dare do it, but I went home to get a hammer and smashed them one by one. I know for sure that nobody saw me, but that evening it turned out that those so-called friends had snitched on me. It was an expensive prank. I received a fine of 5,500 guilders. My stepfather paid it. When I was twelve, the area mental health agency advised my mother to place me on the waiting list for a youth home.

In junior high things didn't get any better. I was teased, usually about my weight. They'd say, "You looking at me, Lumpy?" or "What are you doing here?" Later they didn't have the nerve anymore. I learned to defend myself with my hands. If anybody mouths off at me, I attack them. My class thought it was awesome: cool, some excitement. But I got into more and more fights and after a year I was kicked out of school.

## Brotherhood

I've been at this youth home for three years. I'd rather

live at home, but my mother thinks I should finish my high school education here. I'm going to take my secondary school exams and next year I'm going to get my retailer's diploma. I'd really like to start a small business later on.

My sister has plans for a fitness center and I'll open "Sérgio's Health Shop" downstairs. It'll be a kind of café with a bakery where you can play pool, eat breakfast, and get candy and cake. I think it'd sound awesome to hear people say, "Come on, let's go to Sérgio's."

My family is the most important thing in my life. I have a nice mother who always tries to help me. I'm proudest of my little sister. She cries about everything, but if she has to defend herself, she wins. She has strength inside.

The past few years I've changed. I'm becoming more adult. I became a Jehovah's Witness again, just like my mother and my sister. In Portugal we were Jehovah's Witnesses too. For me, faith is a brotherhood. You learn to get along with people and to restrain yourself better. Everybody's equal and that's the way you should treat one another. There are also things I don't agree with. It doesn't make any sense to me that you can't celebrate your birthday. And what I don't understand is that people can be kicked out of the faith. Then you're not allowed to talk to that person. I think that's ridiculous. If somebody's your friend, he stays your friend, right? When they come up with lines like that, I say "No way" to the Bible. And I just walk.

## The Right One

Later I'd like to have my own family. My girlfriend doesn't have to be super attractive. A sweet and honest personality is the most important thing. I hope we won't have any secrets and that we'll understand each other. A dream relationship, that's what all men want. I'm strict too, having an affair isn't in my book. If I have a girlfriend, I can't be with someone else, it's against my principles. The girl I'm in love with is a Jehovah's Witness too. I hope it turns into something. She does drop hints in that direction, but you never know. Every time I see her, my stomach churns a thousand times a minute. I always hope I'll meet the right one.

# My Number One Wish

**ASENA**
**15, lives on her own**

I know my mother well. I know exactly what she is like, but she doesn't know who I am. The roles are switched around, really. A mother's supposed to know everything about you: when you're sad, what you like to eat, what you think is fun. She's the one you learn everything from. With your mother, you feel safe. But I had to find out on my own. Then you become strong on the outside, but inside you're scared.

## I Am Who I Am

My mother was born in Argentina to Polish-Argentinean parents. When she was fourteen she came to the Netherlands all by herself as a political refugee. Her mother was

active in the resistance to the dictatorship.

I was born when my mother was eighteen. She lived with my father in the Bijlmer high-rises south of Amsterdam. When I was five years old, he went back to Morocco.

My boyfriend thinks it's weird that I don't know my father. He is Turkish and knows thirteen grandfathers. Well, I'm sorry, but I don't know a single father of mine.

I am who I am. I don't feel Moroccan, Polish, or Dutch. Maybe I'm still mostly Argentinean.

## Lived Everywhere

For six months I've been living on my own. Actually I'm still very young, but I have nowhere else to go. I even wanted to go back to a youth home, I didn't care. But my social worker said that he couldn't do anything for me.

I've lived everywhere: with my mother, my uncle, a foster father, a Latin-American family, and at two youth homes. Most recently I lived with a Moroccan foster family. I thought I was OK there. I wanted to educate myself and learn some of the language and culture. We were even planning to go look for my father in Morocco.

In October I left that family. I didn't feel at home there. My foster sister was jealous that I was allowed to do more than she was. But I went through very different things. I decide for myself if I'm going to school, when I come home and leave the house.

## Upside-Down World

If you asked me if I admire my mother, I'd say: I admire that she's still alive. My mother is addicted to heroin. Even when she was pregnant with my little half brother, she kept on. I always kept hoping that she'd quit. That hope keeps you going, but it also breaks you down.

When I was a child, I knew what drugs were. But I didn't understand how bad they are. It was an upside-down world. Others want you to go to school. My mother would ask me to stay home, otherwise she felt so alone. But then, later in the day, she'd leave the house herself. Then I'd be lying in bed waiting for her until the middle of the night. I wondered what I'd done wrong. Friends' parents were crazy about me, why not my own parents?

## A Full Team + Five on Deck

Being a mother is the most beautiful thing there is. I want to spend all my time doing that. My goal is: getting married, having children, that's it. I want sixteen children, a full team and five on deck. I'm still too young for that now. I could manage, I've seen a lot of life, but I want to see more. I've been with my boyfriend for seven months. Things are fine, but you can't predict that we'll spend the rest of our lives together. And I think a child has to have a father and a mother.

My boyfriend is thirty-three years old, over twice my

age. But I feel good with him, safe. I want a serious friend, not a childish relationship. During the day I go to his boutique. I help keep an eye on the shop. At home I'm bored to death. I don't get paid, but he helps me with my rent and that kind of thing. You see, I'm too young to get welfare for myself or rental assistance.

At this point, my boyfriend is all I have. But if we break up, I think I'll make it. I've been alone before. I was able to manage then too.

## Not on My List

I can't change my mother. But that doesn't mean that you have to go the same road. When I was thirteen, I found out that my mother was involved in prostitution. I'd never have thought it. She has such a strong personality. How can she demean herself that way? It's the last thing I'd do. I wouldn't be able to neglect myself like that. Let me put it this way: prostitution is not on my list.

I talked about it with my mother. We got into a fight. She says she really doesn't want to, but that she doesn't have any choice. Of course she does! I could also say, "I can't do anything, this is the only thing," but there are more options. If you really want something else, it'll work out.

I can remember that girls I knew would ask each other if they were still virgins. I didn't know what I was. On the one hand I wasn't a virgin anymore, but I still felt like a virgin, because I hadn't done it voluntarily. I was sexually abused as a child. The first time I was five years old. It was a so-called friend of my mother's. The second time I was eight. He was a contact parent from school. I often stayed overnight at his place. He'd leave his children at his ex-wife's. I felt good with him, he was nice and I liked staying up late. I didn't realize then what was happening. I wanted to protect him. But now I know it was his fault.

## Being Strong

I've never said these things to anybody. I didn't want to let others know that I was weak and that they'd be able to get to me. At school I pretended I was strong. I never had problems with other students, they didn't dare do anything. Once I got into a fight with a girl. I shoved her so hard against the custodian's window that her nose broke. That wasn't my lucky day. I was sent home from school and was only allowed to come back if I apologized. But I didn't regret it. She had said something I can't put up with. She called me a whore.

## Number-One Wish

I'm not in touch with my mother much. I absolutely don't want to be like her. But I have started to be like her. Not in how she acts, but in her way of thinking. That you've had enough of everything.

My boyfriend says there are two Asenas. Sometimes

everything goes well. Then I'm "Happy Asena." But sometimes it switches over. Then I get moody, mad and rude like a child. Now I'm still young, but sometimes I feel like an old woman. Then I'm afraid I won't be able to be happy. That's my number-one wish: to become happy.

# Stories That Need To Be Told

What's it like not growing up with your own parents? If you don't know your mother or father, or if you'd rather not ever see them again. How do you keep going? How do you take care to, as Manuela puts it, "not get dragged down." What do you believe in? What do you wish for, what are your plans and dreams? In 1996 I did interviews for an educational film with a good number of teenagers who couldn't live with their parents (anymore). Impressed by their experiences, I got the idea for this book.

In the summer of 1997, all the kids in *Close-Up* were extensively interviewed. On the basis of their own words I wrote stories. Pieter Kers then made the beautiful photographic portraits.

The teenagers in *Close-Up* talk honestly and in their own way about themselves and their parents. That isn't easy. A couple of them preferred to remain anonymous, and so have not been recognizably photographed.

Why would you cooperate in making a book like this? Why would you entrust your story to somebody you don't know, to an unknown reader who happens to crack the spine of your book?

*Samantha:* "I think it's good for people to know life could also be different. I don't just mean kids, but adults too. A lot of people don't even know, for instance, what foster care is, they just think you're a troublemaker."

*Marco:* "If you look around the train station and you see those homeless people, it makes you think, doesn't it? You wonder what they've gone through. You don't know, but it could be quite something."

Fifteen teens tell their stories in *Close-Up*. Their stories are about trust and betrayal, friendship and grief, fear, resistance and courage. They are stories told by those who often receive attention only when they cause problems. They are stories that need to be told.

*Szabinka Dudevszky*